Love, Piglet

A. A. Milne with decorations by **Ernest H. Shepard**

Dutton Children's Books • New York

Reassurance

Piglet sidled up to Pooh from behind.

"Pooh!" he whispered.

"Yes, Piglet?"

"Nothing," said Piglet, taking Pooh's paw. "I just wanted to be sure of you."

—THE HOUSE AT POOH CORNER

Wishing Pooh Were Here

Piglet put the paper in the bottle, and he corked the bottle up as tightly as he could, and he leant out of his window, and he threw the bottle as far as he could throw; and he watched it floating slowly away in the distance, and then suddenly he knew he had done all that he could to save himself. And then he gave a very long sigh and said, "I wish Pooh were here. It's so much more friendly with two."

—WINNIE-THE-POOH

A Show of Affection

Piglet got up early that morning to pick himself a bunch of violets; and when he had picked them, it suddenly came over him that nobody had ever picked Eeyore a bunch of violets, and the more he thought of this, the more he thought how sad it was to be an Animal who had never had a bunch of violets picked for him.

—THE HOUSE AT POOH CORNER

What If

"If your own house is blown down, you *must* go somewhere else, mustn't you, Piglet? What would *you* do, if *your* house was blown down?"

Before Piglet could think, Pooh answered for him.

"He'd come and live with me," said Pooh, "wouldn't you, Piglet?"

Piglet squeezed his paw.

"Thank you, Pooh," he said, "I should love to."

—THE HOUSE AT POOH CORNER

A Safe Place

"Help, help!" cried Piglet, "a Heffalump, a Horrible Heffalump!" and he scampered off as hard as he could, still crying out, "Help, help, a Herrible Hoffalump! Hoff, Hoff, a Hellible Horralump! Holl, Holl, a Hoffable Hellerump!" And he didn't stop crying and scampering until he got to Christopher Robin's house.

Piglet wasn't afraid if he had Christopher Robin with him.

—WINNIE-THE-POOH

Comfort from Piglet

By and by Pooh and Piglet came along. Pooh was telling Piglet in a singing voice that it didn't seem to matter, if he didn't get any fatter; and Piglet was wondering how long it would be before his haycorn came up.

"Look, Pooh!" said Piglet suddenly. "There's something in one of the Pine Trees."

"So there is!" said Pooh. "There's an Animal."

Piglet took Pooh's arm, in case Pooh was frightened.

—THE HOUSE AT POOH CORNER

Pooh and Piglet's Spot

Half way between Pooh's house and Piglet's house was a Thoughtful Spot where they met sometimes when they had decided to go out and see each other, and as it was warm and out of the wind they would sit down there for a little and wonder what they would do now that they *had* seen each other.

—THE HOUSE AT POOH CORNER

Falling

"Piglet!" cried Pooh eagerly. "Where are you?"

"Underneath," said Piglet in an underneath sort of way.

"Underneath what?"

"You," squeaked Piglet. "Get up!"

"I didn't mean to," said Pooh sorrowfully.

"I didn't mean to be underneath," said Piglet sadly. "But I'm all right now, Pooh, and I *am* so glad it was you."

—THE HOUSE AT POOH CORNER

A Song of Love

"Piglet," said Pooh a little shyly.

"Yes, Pooh?"

"Do you remember when I said that a Respectful Pooh Song might be written about You Know What?"

"Did you, Pooh?" said Piglet, getting a little pink round the nose. "Oh, yes, I believe you did."

"It's been written, Piglet."

And Pooh hummed it to him, all the seven

verses and Piglet said nothing, but just stood and glowed.

—THE HOUSE AT POOH CORNER

Pooh and Piglet walked home thoughtfully together in the golden evening, and for a long time they were silent.

—WINNIE-THE-POOH